MY MOM IS SO UNUSUAL

Iris Loewen

illustrated by

Alan Pakarnyk

PEMMICAN
PUBLICATIONS
INC.

Pemmican Publications Inc. gratefully acknowledges the assistance to its publishing program by Manitoba Arts Council and Canada Council.

PRINTED AND BOUND IN CANADA

CANADIAN CATALOGUING IN PUBLICATION DATA

Loewen, Iris, 1951-
  My mom is so unusual

ISBN 0-919143-37-7

I. Pakarnyk, Alan.   II. Title.
PS8573.039M9 1986   jC813'.54   C86-091324-4
PZ7.L639My 1986

PEMMICAN
PUBLICATIONS
INC.

411 - 504 Main Street / Winnipeg, Manitoba / Canada R3B 0B8

For

Talla, my daughter, and all my friends—Mary,
Myra, Cindy, Kass, Tony, Myrna, Carmen,
Heather, Arnold, Sam, Hazel, Jake, Agnes,
Crystal, Armand, George, Gloria, Ivan,
Audrey, Richard L., Bob, Nora, Earl, Robbie,
Lorraine, Elaine, Lillian, Wanda, Adele and
Seraphine—all of whom will find themselves
somewhere in these pages.

Iris

My
Mom is so unusual.
There's nobody like her in
the whole wide world.

My
Mom and I live alone.
That makes our family
different from the
families of most of my
friends.
We like it this way.

In the summertime, we go for long bike rides. We race. I call her the Mamas. She calls me Speedy Gonzales. I let her win so she'll feel good.

We
like to eat at the Broadway
Cafe. I always order a
grilled cheese sandwich,
chips and gravy. My Mom
orders a salad. She says
she won't have chips
because they make her fat.
Then she eats all my chips
when I'm not looking!

My
Mom doesn't dress like
most moms. My friends
think she looks weird.
I get embarrassed. So my
Mom hugs me.
She laughs and says,
"Weird is wonderful!"

Sometimes,
my Mom is scared of the
dark. Can you believe it?!
I have to go sleep with her.

My
Mom likes rock 'n' roll.
She turns the radio up
really loud when her
favorite song is on. We
dance like crazy.

When
my Mom gets mad, she yells
and hollers. I don't worry
because I know she loves
me even when she's mad.
Sometimes, she even
swears. I have to tell her to
calm down. I tell her
swearing isn't nice. I tell her
to say, "Dirty rotten cream
of wheat," instead.
My Mom never stays mad
for long.

My

Mom says I'm a very special
kid. Everyday, she says,
"I love you."
I love her too. I don't know
what she'd do without me!

IRIS LOEWEN has been involved, both in her personal and professional life with Indian and Metis people. She has a young daughter who was the inspiration for this book.

Iris worked as a librarian for the Saskatchewan Indian Cultural College in Saskatoon, where she helped set up one of the finest Native library collections in Canada. She also travelled to schools on various Saskatchewan reserves to conduct storytelling sessions for the students. Later, she worked for the Lac LaRonge Indian Band, training Native librarians, setting up school libraries, and conducting library and storytelling classes.

Iris was born in Mennen, Saskatchewan. She completed her Bachelor of Education at the University of Saskatchewan and plans to pursue a Master's degree at the Univesity of British Columbia in Vancouver.

ALAN PAKARNYK is a Winnipeg animator/illustrator. Having studied Fine Arts at the University of Manitoba, he later animated five segments for *SESAME STREET*, three of which were the Nanabush legends and much of his recent work is in animation.